My First Day of School

P. K. Hallinan

ISBN-13: 978-0-8249-5305-8
ISBN-10: 0-8249-5305-3
Published by Ideals Children's Books
An imprint of Ideals Publications, A Guideposts Company
Nashville, Tennessee
www.idealsbooks.com

Printed and bound in Mexico

Library of Congress CIP Data on file

RRD-Rey_Oct10_7

ideals children's books..
Nashville, Tennessee

My first day of school
I hopped out of bed
And dressed in my best,
From my toes to my head!

This day would be special
From morning till night,
And I had to be certain
To get it just right.

So I ate a big breakfast
For get-up-and-go . . .

Then went off to school
Like the star of the show!

At school there were children
Going every which way,
All shined up like diamonds
For their very first day.

And while some came on buses,
And some came alone,
The teachers were quick
To make us all feel at home.

We gathered in bunches
By the kindergarten door
To find out what nametags
And bookbags were for . . .

And we learned that we never
Could take the wrong bus
Or ever get lost
With our nametags on us.

And then in a flash,
We marched into class.

There were five little tables
With cards marking places,
So everyone knew
Where their own special place was.

And our teacher just smiled
And talked with such care
That all of our fears
Disappeared into air.

We talked about safety
And how to cross streets . . .

We talked about manners
And keeping things neat.

We even discussed
Where the school bathrooms were . . .

And how to determine
A HIS from a HERS.

And then we had brunch
Of crackers and punch!

At recess we played
On gym bars and trikes
Or just strolled around
On the grounds, if we liked.

But once back in class,
We sat down to stay
And finished the business
We'd started that day.

We made paper signs.

We practiced some rhymes.

We even played games using animal names!

And when we were done,
I think we all knew
That learning to learn
Was a great thing to do!

Then filling my cubby
Before going home,
With papers and projects
I'd done on my own . . .

I just felt like crowing,
"I'm nobody's fool!"
'Cause I'd started learning . . .

My first day of school.